PORCUPINE PENNY

written by:
BA BELTHOFF

t

tate publishing
CHILDREN'S DIVISION

Sweet Dreems! .

BA Belthoff

Published by Tate Publishing & Enterprises, LLC
127 E. Trade Center Terrace | Mustang, Oklahoma 73064 USA
1.888.361.9473 | www.tatepublishing.com

Tate Publishing is committed to excellence in the publishing industry. The company reflects the philosophy established by the founders, based on Psalm 68:11,
"The Lord gave the word and great was the company of those who published it."

Book design copyright © 2013 by Tate Publishing, LLC. All rights reserved.
Cover and interior design by Rhezette Fiel
Illustrations by Katie Brooks

Published in the United States of America

ISBN: 978-1-62854-836-5
1. Juvenile Fiction / Bedtime & Dreams
2. Juvenile Fiction / Family / General
13.09.25

To E and G,

You are my inspiration.

BAB

"That was a nice story, wasn't it?" Daddy asked.

Penny really hadn't been listening. She was thinking about being in her own bed, in her own room—all alone.

Mama and Daddy kissed her good night. "Sleep well, sweet pea. We love you!"

Penny lay awake for what seemed like hours. She twisted and turned. She flipped, and she flopped. She tossed and tumbled. She scooched, and she squirmed. Finally, she got up and tiptoed into her big sister's room.

"Can I sleep in your bed, Sissy?" Penny whispered in Emma's ear.

"What's the matter with your bed?" groaned Emma.

"My bed isn't as comfy as yours," said Penny.

"Arrgh!" groaned Penny's big sister, as she rolled over to make room for Penny.

Penny climbed in the other side. She tried hard to lay still. She loved her sister and didn't want to wake her but...she twisted and turned. She flipped, and she flopped. She tossed and tumbled. She scooched, and she squirmed.

"Sniff, sniff, sniff." Sissy liked to roll in flowers, and now the sweet scent filled the room. Penny tried not to think about it, but...

"*AAACHOOO!*"

She sneezed.

"Errrr," Emma moaned.

Penny sniffed, snuffled, and scratched.

"*Out!*" exclaimed Emma.

Penny got up and tiptoed as quietly as she could across the hall to the room where her grandmother was sleeping. Penny could hear her grandmother's light snore. She thought she was asleep, so she wriggled into Grandma's bed as gently as she could. If only she could fall asleep.

The moon seemed so bright shining through the windows of her grandmother's room. She twisted and turned. She flipped, and she flopped. She tossed and tumbled. She scooched, and she squirmed. But still, the moon shined in her eyes.

"Penny, dear," Grandma whispered, "you can't sleep here if you are going to toss and turn all night."

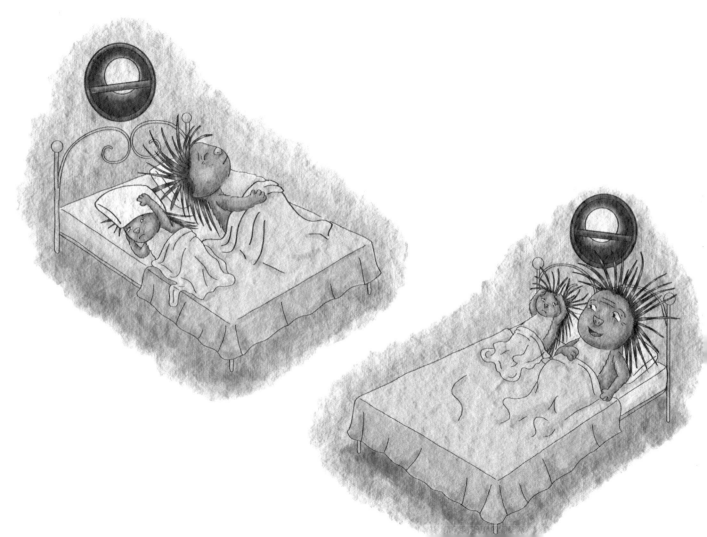

This time, Penny tiptoed down the hall to her parents' room. Very quietly, Penny whispered in her mama's ear.

"Can I sleep in your bed?"

"Penny, you should have been born to an owl family," Mama said. "You never want to go to sleep at night."

"*Please*, Mama, just this once," Penny pleaded.

Penny climbed into her parents' bed. It was big and squishy and warm. She settled in between her mom and dad. But she just couldn't get comfy. She turned right.

"Ouch!" She complained, getting poked by one of Mama's quills. She turned left, rolling into one of Papa's quills. "Ouch!"

"Lay still," Mama said.

Penny just couldn't get comfortable. She twisted and turned. She flipped, and she flopped. She tossed and tumbled. She scooched, and she squirmed. And boy, was it getting warm! Penny lowered the blankets as gently as she could.

"I'm sorry, Penny. You cannot sleep here," Daddy said.

Sadly and sleepily, Penny and her mama walked down the hall.

"Where can I sleep, Mama?" Penny asked with a sigh. "Sissy's room smells like lavender, and the moon is too bright in Grandma's room. Your bed is too hot and…"

Mama whispered, "I know just the place."

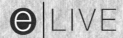

e|LIVE

---

listen|imagine|view|experience

AUDIO BOOK DOWNLOAD INCLUDED WITH THIS BOOK!

In your hands you hold a complete digital entertainment package. In addition to the paper version, you receive a free download of the audio version of this book. Simply use the code listed below when visiting our website. Once downloaded to your computer, you can listen to the book through your computer's speakers, burn it to an audio CD or save the file to your portable music device (such as Apple's popular iPod) and listen on the go!

How to get your free audio book digital download:

1. Visit www.tatepublishing.com and click on the e|LIVE logo on the home page.
2. Enter the following coupon code:
   173d-a90a-962c-8d2d-da21-8ebc-05ee-3cea
3. Download the audio book from your e|LIVE digital locker and begin enjoying your new digital entertainment package today!